AF268898

This project was a labour of love, done in collaboration, not in isolation.
I want to thank each of you who shared your insights, late night chats and support
to make this book a reality. This is for each of you, and for my favourite beings
to bubble with ~ Layla, Myles, Bella & Corey.

Once Upon a Pandemic, A Pregnancy Journey

Written by: Dr. Sheila Wijayasinghe
Illustrated by: Anna Despina Koprantzelas
Book Design & Editing: Corey Tucker

Published by: Bella Books, Toronto Canada
Printed by Amazon

ISBN: 978-1-7776749-1-5

Written by
Dr Sheila Wijayasinghe

Illustrated by
Anna Despina Koprantzelas

ONCE UPON A PANDEMIC

When we found out we were parents-to-be
waves of joy flowed over our family.

The positive news brought so much delight,
and though it was early, we felt your might.

So we planned and prepared, eagerly awaiting your arrival,
then the world went topsy-turvy and we focused on survival.

The more we feared, worried and became disconnected,
the more we were determined to keep you safe, loved, and protected.

Sometimes we felt lost, and often quite unsure.
We checked the news daily, as we all hoped for a cure.

Would you be ok? Would we be ok? Just so much was unknown.
And while we were all in this together, we still felt quite alone.

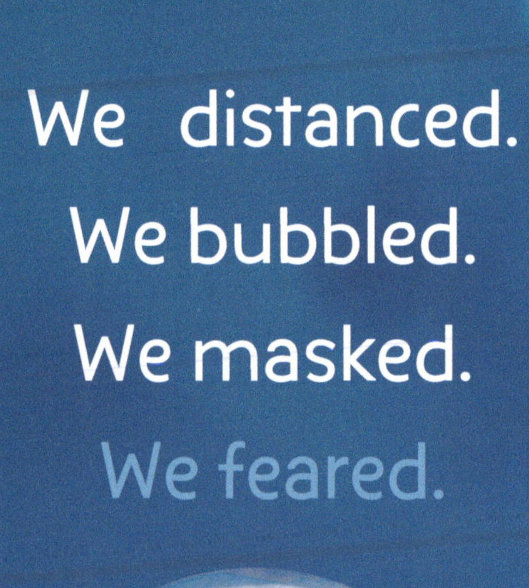

We distanced.
We bubbled.
We masked.
We feared.

We went to appointments alone,
and heard first heartbeats through our phone.

Distanced from friends and saw everyone from afar,
met for porch visits and drive-by parties by car.

Words like zoom and bubbles took on new meaning
and we all practiced our quarantining.

We cheered and gave thanks to all our frontline workers,
grocery clerks, postal carriers, nurses and teachers.
They helped us keep connected, cared for, fed, and taught.
putting themselves at risk, without a second thought.

THANKS!

We distanced.
We bubbled.
We masked.
We persevered.

HOSPITAL

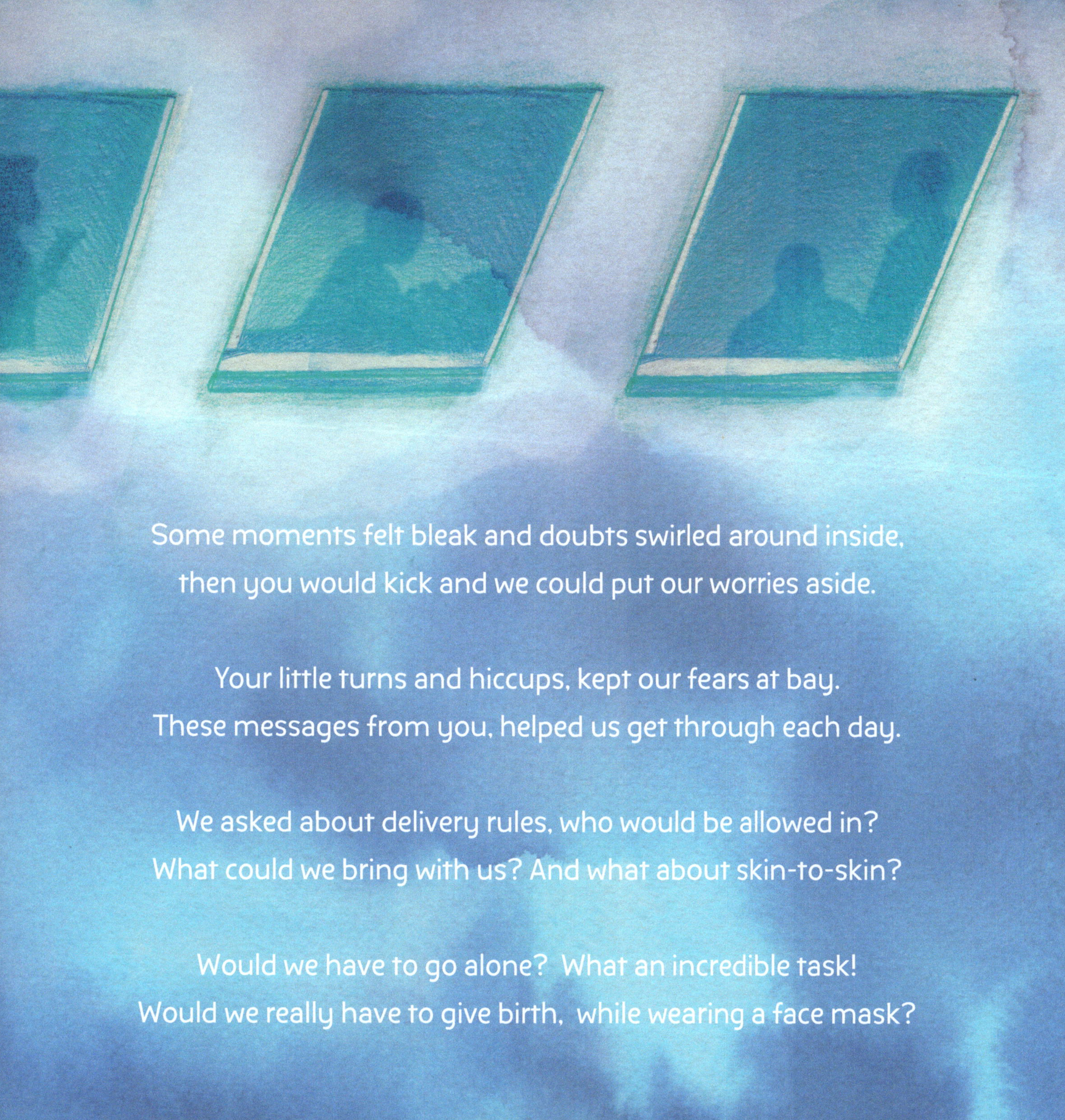

Some moments felt bleak and doubts swirled around inside,
then you would kick and we could put our worries aside.

Your little turns and hiccups, kept our fears at bay.
These messages from you, helped us get through each day.

We asked about delivery rules, who would be allowed in?
What could we bring with us? And what about skin-to-skin?

Would we have to go alone? What an incredible task!
Would we really have to give birth, while wearing a face mask?

We distanced.
We bubbled.
We masked.
We breathed.

When you finally arrived, on that joyful day,
you roared into our world, warrior heart on display.

Our fears melted away when we heard your little cries.
We could not get enough of you and your bright eyes.

You met our loved ones through masks, and even though you could not see,
their smiles were so wide, to meet the newest member of our family.
The return home was quiet without the usual visitor flow.
You met your family through phone, video and sometimes a window.

Not having people over, was honestly quite tough.
Without the extra hands and hugs, would we be enough?
But we learned quick with coaching from a distance
and we got through your early days with love and persistence.

We distanced.
We bubbled.
We masked.
We loved.

Now you are here and the world has a little more brilliance.

This bumpy start was tough, but showed us our resilience.

There will always be ups and downs and other storms to weather,

but now we know, we can get through anything together.

Though this journey to you was different than expected,

we will always keep you safe, loved, and protected.

Even on the most difficult days, one thing always stayed true:

We would do it over again, because it brought us to you.

About the Author

Dr. Sheila Wijayasinghe is a family doctor in Toronto. She lives in Leslieville with her husband Corey and two children, Layla and Myles, and pup Bella. You can follow her at @DrSheilaW on Instagram and Twitter.

About the Illustrator

Anna Despina Koprantzelas is an Italian illustrator. She lives and works in her house in the countryside near Verona with her two little bunnies.